For Don Wood

HBJ

Copyright © 1993 by Audrey Wood

Requests for permission to make copies of any part of
the work should be mailed to: Permissions Department,
Harcourt Brace Jovanovich, Publishers, 8th Floor, Orlando, Florida 32887.

Library of Congress Cataloging-in-Publication Data
Wood, Audrey.
Rude giants/by Audrey Wood.
p.   cm.
Summary: Beatrix the butter maid saves Gerda the cow
and transforms two rude giants into good neighbors.
ISBN 0-15-269412-9
[1. Giants — Fiction. 2. Neighborliness — Fiction.
3. Behavior — Fiction.] I. Title.
PZ7.W846Ru   1993
[E] — dc20   91-13015

First edition   A B C D E

Printed in Singapore

The illustrations in this book were done in watercolor, gouache,
and colored pencil on medium-weight watercolor paper.
The text type was set in Adroit Light
by Thompson Type, San Diego, California.
Color separations by Bright Arts, Ltd., Singapore
Printed and bound by Tien Wah Press, Singapore
Production supervision by Warren Wallerstein and Ginger Boyer
Designed by Camilla Filancia

RUDE GIANTS

Harcourt Brace Jovanovich, Publishers

San Diego   New York   London

Long ago, Beatrix the butter maid and her best friend, Gerda the cow, lived in a cozy cottage in a happy valley.

Every morning after tea, Beatrix served Gerda the freshest yellow hay, and Gerda gave Beatrix the sweetest milk to make into butter and sell at the market.

The girl and the cow never had a care in the world until
the day . . .

. . . two rude giants came over the mountains and moved into the empty castle on the hill.

The rude giants were clumsy, loud, and selfish. They trampled the flowers, quarreled until the birds stopped singing, and stole whatever they wanted from whomever they pleased.

What will those rude giants do next? the villagers wondered.

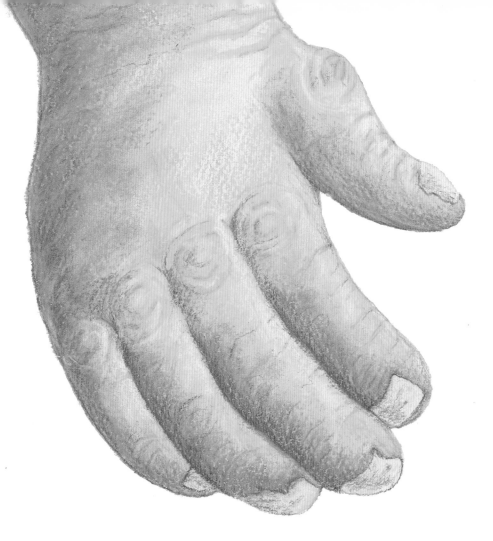

But life must go on, giants or not. So, on market day, as usual, Beatrix the butter maid and Gerda the cow set off for the market to sell their butter. They hadn't traveled far when a great hand reached down and scooped Gerda up into the sky.

"Yum!" the giantess bellowed. "Food!"

Beatrix jumped onto one of the giant's shoes and held on tight. Thump! Thump! Thump! In three giant steps the giantess returned to the castle and tossed Gerda onto a table before her husband.

Quickly the butter maid climbed up the table leg and pulled herself onto the top.

"Stop!" Beatrix exclaimed. "You can't eat the finest cow in all the land!"

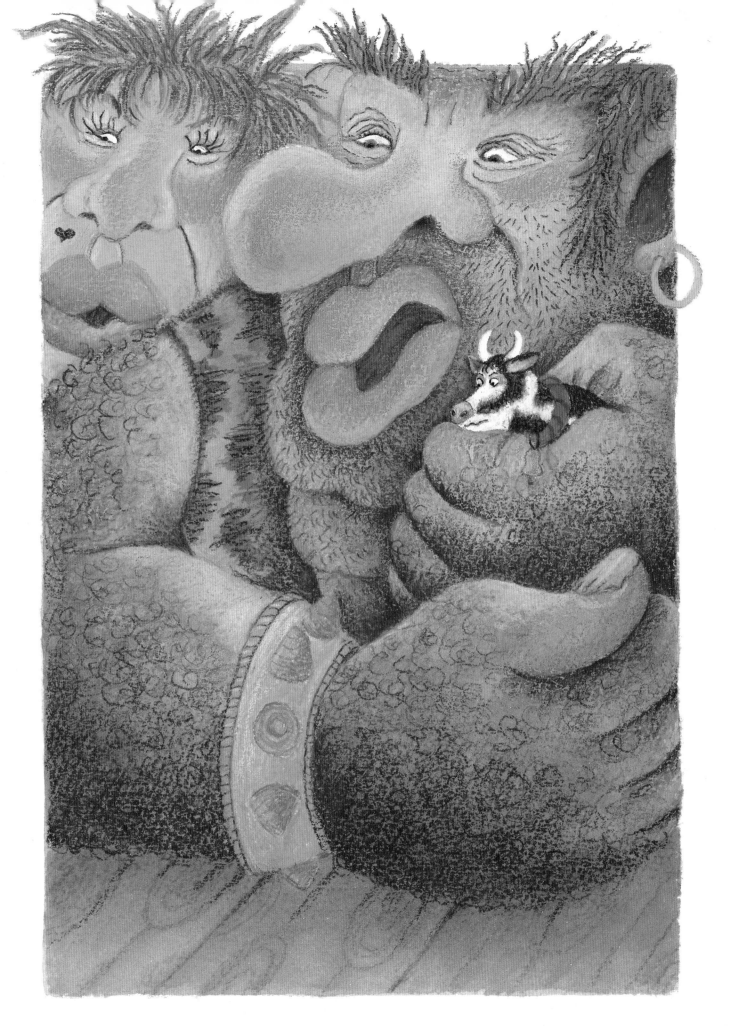

"Huh?" the rude giant said. "Why not?"

"Because," the butter maid answered, "you don't know how to make her taste delicious."

"Tell us how!" the rude giants shouted.

"Why, just look at this messy place," Beatrix scolded. "Everyone knows a good meal tastes better in a clean castle."

"Clean?" the giants said. "What's that?"

Beatrix the butter maid told the giants what to do.
They swept and scrubbed, junked the junk, and put
everything back in its proper place.

The rude giants worked so hard they were hungrier than ever.
"Cow!" they bellowed, reaching for Gerda. "We want cow!"
"Moo!" Gerda cried.

"Stop!" Beatrix exclaimed. "How can you think about eating the finest cow in all the land if you don't have manners? Everyone knows a lack of manners ruins a good meal."

"Manners?" the rude giants shouted. "Show us manners or we'll squish you flat!"

Beatrix the butter maid told the giants what to do. They learned how to speak in pleasant voices,

take tiny bites,

and sip, not slurp.

Boom! Boom! Boom! The giants' stomachs rumbled like
thunder beyond the mountains.

"We eat cow now!" they shouted, forgetting their manners.
The rude giants reached for Gerda.

"Moo! Moo!" Gerda cried.

"Not yet!" Beatrix the butter maid exclaimed. "If you are going to eat the finest cow in all the land, there's still one more thing you must do to make her taste delicious."

"Tell us, please!" the rude giants said, trying to be polite. "Oh please, tell us!"

"You must make yourselves beautiful," the butter maid said.

"Beautiful!" the giants exclaimed. "What's that?"

"Give Gerda to me," Beatrix said, "and we will show you."

The butter maid and the cow worked together. They filled a tub with water and told the giants how to take a bubble bath.

They curled and combed
the giants' hair in fancy ways.
Then they sewed the softest
cloth into lovely outfits.

"Now just look at yourselves," the butter maid said. "How could two beautiful giants like you, who live in a clean castle and have good manners, eat my dear friend Gerda the cow?"

The giants peered into a mirror. They couldn't believe
their eyes.

The giantess fluttered her long eyelashes and smiled sweetly.

The giant smoothed back his glistening hair and raised one giant eyebrow.

"My dear," he said to his giant wife, "you look simply divine."

"And you," she said to her giant husband, "look handsome indeed!"

"Moo," Gerda said in her sweetest voice.

The giants looked at the cow. Their giant stomachs growled as they licked their giant lips.

Bending down low, they whispered in the butter maid's ear, "Hungry, we are still very H-U-N-G-R-Y! What are we to do?"

Beatrix knew what to do. She left the castle, hurried to the village, and rang the bells.

From far and near the villagers gathered around.

That evening, as the sun set behind the mountains, the butter maid led the villagers up the path to the giants' castle.

Everyone brought something from home. With a pot of this and a jug of that, there was plenty for all.

"From now on," the giant proclaimed, "we'll have a party every week."

"And all our friends are invited," the giantess agreed.

Now the giants were very happy. In time they had a giant baby.
Much to their surprise, the child soon grew to be ruder than
they had ever been. Of course, they knew what to do. The
giants sent their rude child to the finest teachers in all the
land . . .

. . . Beatrix the butter maid and Gerda the cow.

The Complete Book of
DRAWING
TECHNIQUES

A PROFESSIONAL GUIDE FOR THE ARTIST

Peter Stanyer

BARNES
&NOBLE
BOOKS
NEW YORK